WATER BOY

David McPhail

ABRAMS BOOKS FOR YOUNG READERS
NEW YORK

Cataloging-in-Publication Data has been applied for and may be obtained
from the Library of Congress.

ISBN 13: 978-0-8109-1784-2
ISBN 10: 0-8109-1784-X

Text and illustrations copyright © 2007 David McPhail

Book design by Chad W. Beckerman
Production Manager: Alexis Mentor

Published in 2007 by Abrams Books for Young Readers,
an imprint of Harry N. Abrams, Inc.

Printed and bound in Hong Kong
10 9 8 7 6 5 4 3 2 1

harry n. abrams, inc.
a subsidiary of La Martinière Groupe
115 West 18th Street
New York, NY 10011
www.hnabooks.com

For my grandson, whose sense of wonder
and amazement rivals my own.
With love,

P. D.

"You are water," the boy's teacher told him, ". . . mostly." This information fascinated the boy, though at the same time he found it a bit unsettling. He wondered what would happen to him.

Would he dissolve in the rain?

Or turn to ice in the winter?

If his cat scratched him, would all that water leak out and leave him lying flat on the sidewalk like a punctured balloon?

Ever since the bathwater wrapped around his big toe and tried to pull him down the drain, the boy had been a reluctant bather.

So he refused to take a bath at all, and when his mother asked why, he told her what the teacher had said.

"Water is part of all of us," his mother explained, trying to comfort him. "It's a good thing. We cannot live without it."

After that, the boy was less afraid, and though he did resume bathing, he clung to the sides of the tub the whole time.

As the days went by, water became more and more like
a friend to the boy. When it rained, he put on his boots
and went outside to play in the puddles. And if it didn't
rain, he would fill up his boots with water and slosh
around the house, until his mother told him to stop.

The boy was visiting his grandmother when she asked him what his favorite color was.

"Blue," he replied.

So she knitted him a sweater the color of the ocean on a cloudless afternoon. He wore it nearly every day.

Strange things began to happen. One evening, as he was helping with the dishes, the water from the faucet curled into letters that spelled his name.

As he walked along the beach near his home, the seabirds encircled the boy and brought him treasures.

When he stood on the cliffs, the waves sang to him.

In the bath, the boy could push all of the water to one end of the tub, where it would stay until he nodded his head.

It was a trick that came in handy on a school field trip to a world-famous waterfall, when a little dog fell into the water and was in danger of being swept away.

And at the pond in the park, when his sailboat tipped over and began to sink, a waterspout picked it up, carried it back across the pond, and gently placed it at the boy's feet.

The boy spent a lot of time practicing water tricks.

After much trial and error, he was able to toss water from a glass and have it come snapping back, like a yo-yo.

But the boy's favorite trick was to balance a drop of water on the tip of his finger. When he held it up close, he could see everything that lay at the bottom of the ocean.

The boy discovered that he could squeeze gallons of rainwater into an old baby-food jar.

He placed the jar on his windowsill so the water could absorb energy from the sun.

He conducted experiments.

The boy found that just one drop of water from the jar could clear up a bottle of the densest ink. Two drops would clean a large mud puddle.

He took the jar to school one day to demonstrate the water's strange power. On his way home, the boy was crossing a bridge when he heard a voice calling for help.

The boy looked around.

He was alone.

Then he heard the cry again.

He looked over the side of the bridge. There was no one there. The cry was from the river, begging to be made clean.

The boy removed the jar from his school bag and carefully poured out one gleaming drop. When it splashed into the river, that single drop formed a sparkling blue ring that rippled steadily outward.

The boy poured another drop, then another.

Now the shimmering ripples reached from bank to bank.

Slowly the boy emptied out the entire jar and watched as the river ran clear all the way to the ocean and beyond.

Later, as the boy walked along the
shore, a bottle washed up at his feet.

Inside the bottle was a note with his name on it.

"Thank you," the note said.

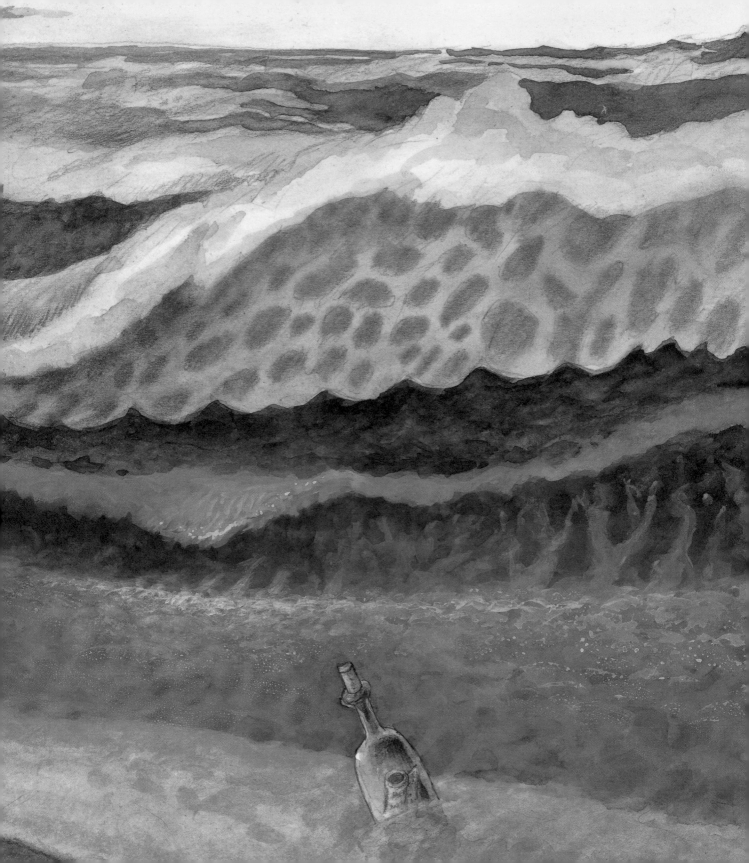

The boy slipped the note into his pocket and continued on home.

His bath would be waiting.